Megan
the Monday
Fairy

by Daisy Meadows

illustrated by Georgie Ripper

ORCHARD BOOKS

www.rainbowmagic.co.uk

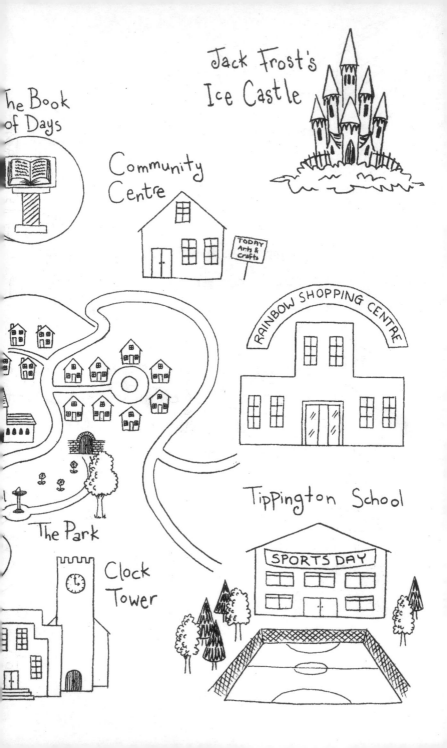

Icy wind now fiercely blow!
To the Time Tower I must go.
Goblin servants follow me
And steal the Fun Day Flags I need.

I know there will be no fun,
For fairies or humans once the flags are gone.
So, storm winds, take me where I say.
My plan for chaos starts today!

Contents

The Fairies Send Francis

"I'm glad I'm staying with you for half-term," Kirsty Tate told her friend, Rachel Walker, as they came out of Fashion Fun, the accessories shop on Tippington High Street. "And I hope these sparkly clips will look nice with my new hairstyle!"

"I'm sure they will," Rachel said

cheerfully. "They're so pretty."

"Thanks," Kirsty replied. "I wonder how the fairies are," she added, lowering her voice.

Rachel and Kirsty shared a magical secret: when they had first met on a very special holiday to Rainspell Island, they had become friends with the fairies!

"I hope Jack Frost and his goblins are behaving themselves," Rachel said.

Cold, spiteful Jack Frost and his mean goblin servants often caused trouble for the fairies, and the girls had helped their tiny friends outwit Jack Frost many times.

"Look, Rachel!" Kirsty said, peering
into a nearby window. "This shop wasn't
open last time I was here. Isn't it lovely?"

The shop was called Dancing Days,
and the window was full of dance
costumes and dancing shoes. There
were white tutus with gauzy net skirts,
satin ballet slippers with pink ribbons
and sparkly tap shoes.

"I'd love to be able to tap dance," said
Rachel.

Just then the shop door opened and
a lady emerged, followed by a girl with
long brown hair in a ponytail.

The girl's face lit up
when she saw Rachel.
"Hi, Rachel!" she called.
"Hi, Karen," said
Rachel with a smile.
"Kirsty, this is Karen.
She's a friend from
school. And this is her mum."

Karen grinned at Kirsty. "It's nice to
meet you," she said. "Rachel talks about
you all the time!"

Kirsty laughed. "Are you learning to
dance?" she asked, glancing at Karen's
blue bag.

"Yes," Karen replied. "I've got my tap class at the town hall this afternoon and Mum's just bought me some new tap shoes. My old ones were worn out."

"That's because she practises so much!" Mrs Lewis said, smiling. She glanced at her watch. "We'd better hurry, Karen."

"See you later!" Karen called as they left.

"Maybe you could sign up for Karen's tap classes," Kirsty suggested to Rachel as they walked down the street.

"Good idea," Rachel agreed. "Shall we walk home through the park?"

"OK," Kirsty replied.

The girls walked through the iron gates and across the grass. The borders were bright with colourful flowers, and in the middle of the garden was a large brass sundial shining in the sun.

"The sun's bright today," Kirsty said.

Rachel nodded. Then she noticed something that made her heart beat faster: tiny golden sparkles were hovering and dancing above the sundial!

"Kirsty, look at the sundial!" Rachel gasped. "I think it's fairy magic!"

Kirsty's eyes widened. Rachel was right. And now the golden sparkles were moving. As the girls watched, the fairy dust drifted down to circle around a tiny door in the base of the sundial.

Rachel frowned. "I've seen this sundial hundreds of times, but I've never noticed a door before," she said. Suddenly the little door burst open and a frog hopped out. He wore a smart red waistcoat and a gold pocket watch. "Hello, Rachel. Hello, Kirsty," he croaked. The girls beamed at him. "You must be from Fairyland!" Rachel guessed.

The frog nodded. "I'm Francis, the Royal Time Guard," he explained. "I'm a friend of Bertram's." The girls had met Bertram, the frog footman, during their fairy adventures.

"Is everything OK?" Kirsty asked.

Francis shook his head, looking sad. "The King and Queen of Fairyland need your help!" he croaked. "Will you come?"

"Yes, of course!" Rachel and Kirsty chorused.

"Thank you, girls," Francis beamed. He reached into his pocket and pulled out some fairy dust which he threw into the air.

Immediately a dazzling rainbow,
shimmering with colour, began to rise
up from the ground.

"Follow me," said Francis, hopping
into the end of the rainbow.

Rachel and Kirsty both stepped
carefully into the rainbow beside Francis.

"Now off we go!" he said with
a smile, and, in a shower of sparkles,
the rainbow whizzed them all away
to Fairyland.

The Time Tower

In the blink of an eye, Kirsty and
Rachel found themselves in
Fairyland, and transformed into
fairies with glittering wings on their
backs. In front of them stood the
silver palace with its four pink
towers, and King Oberon and
Queen Titania.

The King and Queen were
surrounded by a group of fairies, but
both Rachel and Kirsty could see that
they all looked very unhappy. The girls
wondered why.

Francis jumped out of the end of
the rainbow and bowed to the King
and Queen. "Your Majesties," he

announced as the girls stepped out of the rainbow too. "Here are our good friends, Kirsty and Rachel!"

Queen Titania hurried forwards, a welcoming smile on her face. "It's very good of you to come, girls," she said. "We really need your help!"

"What's happened?" asked Rachel.

"Is it Jack Frost?" Kirsty added.

Queen Titania nodded. "Jack Frost has stolen the Fun Day Flags!" she sighed. "And now the Fun Day Fairies can't get on with their job of making every day in Fairyland and the human world fun."

Rachel and Kirsty glanced at the fairies. They looked very miserable and their wings drooped.

"These are our Fun Day Fairies," said King Oberon. "Megan the Monday Fairy, Talullah the Tuesday Fairy, Willow the Wednesday Fairy, Thea the Thursday Fairy, Freya the Friday Fairy, Sienna the Saturday Fairy and Sarah the Sunday Fairy."

The fairies managed to smile at Rachel and Kirsty, but they still looked sad. The girls felt sorry for them.

"How do the Fun Day Flags work?" asked Kirsty.

"Come with us to the golden pool," Queen Titania replied, "and we'll show you."

The Queen led the way through the palace gardens to the magic pool. They all clustered round it and the Queen waved her wand over the pool. Immediately the water began to shimmer with fairy magic.

"Today Francis the Royal Time Guard went to the Book of Days to check which day it was, just as he does every morning," Queen Titania said, pointing at the pool. "The Book of Days is kept in the Time Tower, on the other side of the palace gardens."

Rachel and Kirsty watched as
a gleaming white marble tower
appeared on the surface of
the pool. The tower had
a golden flagpole on top,
and there was a beautiful
grassy courtyard to one
side of it, full of orange
and lemon trees. In
the middle of the
courtyard's grassy floor
was a giant clock,
made of dazzling
white and gold tiles.
In the pictures in the
pool, the girls saw Francis
hop inside the tower and over to
a large, leather-bound book which
sat on a rainbow-coloured pedestal.

"That's the Book of Days," the
Queen explained. "It keeps track of
the days of the week in case Francis
ever forgets."

As Rachel and Kirsty watched,
Francis left the book and went over to
a golden cabinet at the side of the
room. He took out some bright red
material and unfolded it.

"It's a flag," said Rachel.

"It's beautiful!" added Kirsty.

The flag was large and rectangular, with a large sun surrounded by rays in the middle of it. The sun was the same red colour as the rest of the flag, but it was made of a sparkling fabric that glittered in the sunlight which streamed in through the windows of the Time Tower.

"That's my Monday Fun Flag," said a miserable voice.

Rachel and Kirsty glanced at Megan the Monday Fairy. She wore a dark blue dress with a broad red sash, and her long, glossy black hair was held back by a red Alice band. She looked like she should be laughing and full of fun, but her face was sad.

In the images in the pool, Francis had climbed to the top of the Time Tower and was attaching the Monday Fun Flag to the flagpole.

"Do you see Megan waiting down in the courtyard?" asked Queen Titania as the picture changed. Megan was standing in the middle of the tiled clock, at the point where the two hands met. She had her wand in her hand and she was gazing up at the flag.

"When the sun's rays reflect off the shiny parts of the flag, magical sparkles stream down to the spot where Megan is waiting," Queen Titania explained. "This is how the Fun Day Fairies recharge their wands, to make sure that they have enough magic for their special day."

"It takes a lot of magic to make sure humans can have fun for a whole day!" Megan added.

Kirsty and Rachel watched as Francis ran the flag to the top of the flagpole. Down in the courtyard, Megan raised her wand.

But just as the sunshine was about to hit the flag, there was a sudden gust of fierce wind. Rachel and Kirsty gasped as they saw Jack Frost whizzing towards the

flagpole, propelled by the blast. He snatched the Monday Fun Flag from the flagpole, and zoomed away, cackling triumphantly!

A Clever Clue

"Oh, no!" Rachel cried.

"Poor Megan," said Kirsty, putting her arm around the fairy.

"That's not all," Megan sighed, pointing to the pool. "Look…"

As Francis hurried down from the flagpole, some of Jack Frost's goblin servants appeared and dashed inside the tower.

Quickly they pulled open the golden cabinet where the Fun Day Flags were kept.

"Let's take all the Fun Day Flags!" shouted one.

"Yes, then we can have fun," another yelled gleefully. "And nobody else will!"

The goblins began grabbing the flags from the golden cabinet.

"Stop!" shouted Francis, hopping through the doorway. He tried to pull one of the flags away from the goblin nearest to him. "Give those back!"

"No way!" the goblins chuckled. They rushed for the door, whooping loudly and waving the flags triumphantly. Poor Francis was bundled aside as they charged out of the Time Tower.

"Poor Francis!" Rachel exclaimed, as the pictures in the pool began to fade. "So the goblins stole all the flags!"

Queen Titania nodded. "But Jack Frost doesn't have them anymore," she said with a smile. "Watch what happened…" And she waved her wand over the pool again.

Rachel and Kirsty watched as a new picture appeared. It showed Jack Frost's ice castle. Three goblins were sliding down the frozen banisters of the grandstaircase, squealing with delight. Four goblins were playing hide and seek, one of them peeping out from behind Jack Frost's ice throne. Other goblins were playing football with a solid ball of ice, and some were skating on the icy floor of the throne room, doing twists and turns and jumps.

"The goblins are having fun!" Kirsty laughed.

"That's the power of the Fun Day Flags," explained Megan.

Now the picture changed again to show Jack Frost stomping angrily down the corridor towards his bedroom. "Will you stop having fun and get on with some work?" he shouted at his goblin servants.

Rachel and Kirsty's eyes widened as Jack Frost opened the bedroom door and a stream of warm water cascaded over him from above.

"Help!" Jack Frost yelled, dancing around in fury. "I'm soaked!"

A second later a bucket tumbled down from on top of the door and fell over his head, muffling his voice. Rachel and Kirsty laughed. Meanwhile, the goblins who had set up the trick were peeping round the corner, giggling hysterically.

"That's it!" Jack Frost roared, yanking the bucket off his head. "I'm fed up with all this fun!"

And he raised his wand and shouted
a spell, "Goblins have no time for fun,
so Fun Day Flags, you must be gone!"

Immediately a fierce wind whirled
through the ice palace and, while the
goblins watched in dismay, it whisked
the flags out of the window.

"So where are the flags now?" asked
Rachel, as the pictures faded.

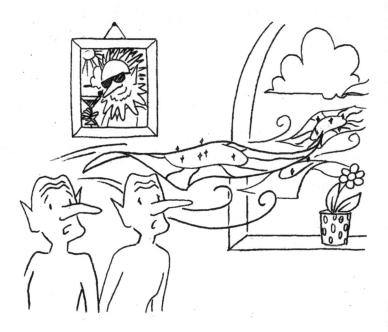

"Jack Frost's spell carried them into the human world where they became bigger," replied Queen Titania. "But the goblins missed the fun they were having so much that some of them sneaked off to look for the flags."

"So we must find the flags before they do," added Megan. "Will you help, girls?"

"Of course we will," said Kirsty.

"Where shall we start?" asked Rachel.

Francis stepped forwards. He took out his pocket watch and opened the lid. Immediately a cloud of magic sparkles swirled out of the watch, and the Book of Days appeared in his hands.

43

"I think there might be a clue in the Book of Days," he croaked, showing one of the pages to Megan, Rachel and Kirsty. "Look, instead of saying what day it is, there's now a poem on the Monday page."

Kirsty read the poem aloud:

"Searching near and searching far,
I know where the Fun Day Flags are.
Look for Monday with the shoes.
Tip and tap are all your clues."

"If we can work out what the poem means, we'll find the flag!" said Rachel excitedly.

"Tip and tap…" Kirsty repeated thoughtfully. "I wonder what that could mean…"

Everyone frowned, thinking hard.

Then, suddenly, Rachel gave a gasp. "Oh!" she said, her eyes shining. "I've got it!"

Finding the Flag

Everyone turned to look eagerly at Rachel.

"Tip and tap!" Rachel said excitedly. "Kirsty, what does that remind you of?"

Kirsty looked blank.

"Remember this morning?" Rachel went on.

Suddenly Kirsty's face lit up. "You mean Karen and her tap dancing lesson!" she cried. "Do you think the Monday flag might be with Karen's new tap shoes?"

Rachel nodded and quickly explained to the fairies and Francis what Kirsty meant. "Karen's lesson is at the town hall this afternoon," she added. "We'd better get there right away!"

"I'll send you there with magic," said Queen Titania, raising her wand.

"I'll come too," Megan announced. "I may not have my Fun Day Magic, but I might still be able to help with my normal fairy magic."

The two girls closed their eyes as Queen Titania showered them with golden fairy dust.

"Good luck!" the other fairies called.

A moment later Kirsty and Rachel could hear the sound of traffic. They opened their eyes and found themselves next to Tippington Town Hall.

"Where's Megan?" asked Rachel.

"Here I am!" declared Megan,

popping out from behind the nearby postbox. She fluttered over to Kirsty's shoulder, hiding herself behind Kirsty's hair.

"There's Karen," Rachel said suddenly, pointing at the town hall steps.

Karen looked very miserable. She was sitting on the steps with her chin in her hands.

"Hi, Karen," called Rachel. "What's wrong?"

"Oh, Rachel," Karen gulped. "Mum dropped me off a bit early for my

class, so I put my bag down while
I was practising some steps. Then, when
I turned round, my bag had gone!"

"Were your new shoes in the bag?"
asked Kirsty.

Karen nodded, biting her lip.

"Oh, I wish I could help Karen
have fun," Megan whispered in
Kirsty's ear, "but I can't without
my Fun Day Magic."

"Here comes my dance teacher, Miss Henry," Karen said tearfully. "I don't want to miss my class."

"Karen, whatever's the matter?" asked Miss Henry, when she saw Karen's miserable face.

Quickly Karen explained.

"You won't miss class because I can lend you a pair of tap shoes for today," Miss Henry said kindly. "And afterwards I'll help you look for your bag."

"And Kirsty and I will look for it while you have your lesson," Rachel added.

"Thanks," Karen said, looking more cheerful as she followed her teacher into the town hall.

Rachel turned to Kirsty and Megan. "Let's start by looking around here," she suggested.

But Kirsty was frowning. "I can hear a strange noise," she whispered.

"So can I," Megan agreed. "It sounds like someone muttering."

Rachel listened too. "It's coming from round the side of the building," she said.

Megan and the girls went over to
the corner and peeped round it.

"It's a goblin!" Kirsty whispered.

"And look what he's holding!"
added Rachel.

The goblin was poking about inside
a blue bag. As Megan and the girls
watched, he began trying to pull a piece
of shiny red material from it.

"That's my flag!" Megan cried.

The goblin got more and more
annoyed as the flag would not come
free. But suddenly he looked up and
saw the girls and Megan watching him.
With a shriek of rage, he grabbed the
bag and ran away.

Clock-watching

"After him!" Megan cried, zooming off in pursuit.

Rachel and Kirsty ran after her. Ahead of them the goblin whizzed round the corner out of sight.

"He's gone round the back of the hall," Kirsty panted.

"That's where the Clock Tower is,"

Rachel puffed, pointing ahead of her.

When the girls and Megan reached the corner, they were just in time to see the goblin dash through the big wooden door at the bottom of the Clock Tower. As they rushed over, the goblin slammed the door shut.

"He's locked it from the inside!" Kirsty exclaimed, trying the handle.

Rachel put her ear to the door. "I think he's going up the stairs," she reported.

"Let's fly to the top and see what he's up to," said Megan, lifting her wand. With a shower of sparkling fairy dust, Megan turned the girls into fairies. Then they all flew to the top of the Clock Tower.

As they arrived the girls could hear the goblin chuckling with glee behind the large white clock face.

"Look," Megan said, pointing at the clock. The minute hand was bouncing up and down. "My Monday Fun Flag means that the goblin's having fun!"

The girls could hear the goblin laughing as he played with the gears controlling the clock's hands. Meanwhile,

the girls zipped round the Clock Tower, looking for a way in. They couldn't find one. "It's no good. There's no way in," sighed Kirsty at last.

"Then we'll just have to get the goblin out!" said Rachel firmly.

"How?" asked Megan.

They all thought hard.

Suddenly, Rachel had an idea. "The clock chimes on the hour," she said. "And it's really loud. It must be even louder inside near the bells. I bet all that noise would drive the goblin out!"

"But it's only a quarter past ten,"
Kirsty pointed out.

"I could use my magic," Megan
said eagerly.

She pointed her wand
at the clock and sent
a stream of fairy
dust towards it.
Immediately, the
hands began to
zoom round towards
the twelve o'clock position.

Bong!

The bells began to chime the hour.
The chimes were so loud that Megan,
Rachel and Kirsty quickly flew back to
the ground to escape the noise.

Bong!

"The goblin won't be able to stand it!"

Kirsty laughed, as Megan waved her wand and turned Rachel and Kirsty back to their usual size.

Bong!

Suddenly the door of the Clock Tower flew open and the goblin rushed out, groaning loudly. He was trying to hang on to Karen's bag and cover his ears at the same time, but the bag kept slipping from his grasp.

Kirsty stepped forwards and caught it
as it fell. "Thank you,"
she said politely.

The goblin didn't
seem to care. "This
is no fun!" he
wailed, and clapping
his hands more firmly
over his ears, he dashed off.

"Look!" Megan said, hovering above
the bag, her face excited. She pointed
her wand at one of the side pockets.
A sparkling piece of red material was
poking out. "Girls, it's my Monday
Fun Flag!"

Time for Fun

Rachel and Kirsty beamed at each other.

"Let's go and give Karen her bag,"
said Rachel, tucking the flag safely under
her arm.

Kirsty and Megan nodded eagerly.

"And then I must get the Monday flag
back to Fairyland," Megan said.

They all went into the town hall

together, with Megan perched on Kirsty's
shoulder. The girls followed the sound of
music coming from a room at the back
of the building, and peered through the
window in the door.

Karen was in the
middle of a group of
girls, tip-tapping their
way across the room.
Miss Henry watched,
shaking her head and
frowning. Karen and the
other girls didn't look very happy either.

"We'll try that again," Miss Henry said
glumly, stopping the music. "You all
seem to have forgotten the steps."

One girl sighed loudly. "I just can't get
them right," she said.

"Neither can I," put in another.

66

"No-one's having any fun," Megan whispered to Kirsty. "And I can't help until I've recharged my wand with Monday magic!"

Suddenly, Karen noticed Rachel and Kirsty at the door. A big smile lit up her face when she saw the bag in Kirsty's hand. She dashed over and flung the door open. "Thank you! Where was it?" she asked.

"Round the side of the town hall," Rachel told her.

"However did it get there?" Karen asked, but luckily she didn't wait for an answer – she was too busy pulling the bag open and taking out her sparkly new tap shoes.

"They're lovely!" Kirsty said, as
Karen quickly took off her
borrowed shoes and
put on the new ones.

"Maybe I'll dance
better now," said
Karen, smiling.
"I can't seem to get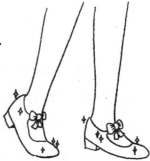
any of the steps right today." She
waved at the girls as she hurried back
to join the class. "Thanks so much!"

"I must get back to Fairyland to
recharge my wand," Megan said
urgently. "Do you want to come?"

The girls nodded and Megan lifted her
wand. In a shower of magic fairy dust,
they were all whisked off to Fairyland.

King Oberon, Queen Titania, Francis
and the Fun Day Fairies were waiting

outside the Time Tower. They all
cheered as Megan, Rachel and Kirsty
appeared with the Monday flag, now
fairy flag-sized again, in Rachel's hand.

"Well done!" called King Oberon
delightedly. "Francis, please fly the flag!"

Francis took the flag from Rachel and
rushed inside the Time Tower.

Meanwhile Megan zoomed over to
the tiled clock in the middle of the
courtyard and stood at the point where
the hands met. She raised her wand
high and waited.

Rachel and Kirsty held their breath as they watched Francis run the Monday Fun Flag to the top of the flagpole. As it reached the top, the golden rays of the

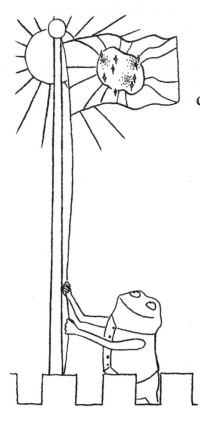

sun struck the flag. Rachel and Kirsty gasped as a beam of dazzling sunlight was reflected right down into the courtyard towards Megan. The golden light hit the tip of Megan's wand, which immediately sparkled with a magical red glow. Everyone clapped and cheered.

"Hurrah!" Megan cried, dancing
with joy. "Now I can put the fun back
into Monday!"

Rachel and Kirsty rushed to join her.

"Thank you, girls!" called Queen
Titania as everyone shouted goodbye.

Megan lifted her wand and, in
a sparkling flash, whisked
herself and the girls
back to the corridor
outside Karen's
dance class. Peeping
through the
window, they saw
one girl accidentally
bump into Karen
and nearly send her
flying. Everyone still
looked glum.

"Time for some Monday fun!" Megan whispered.

Rachel and Kirsty watched as the little fairy poked the tip of her wand through the keyhole of the door. A stream of red sparkles drifted into the room and swirled around the dancers, but they were all too busy concentrating on their steps to notice.

"Stop, girls!" called Miss Henry suddenly, switching off the CD player with a smile. "I have an idea!" She went over to a cupboard and dragged out a large cardboard box. "I was going to save these for later, but I think it would be fun to use them now…"

"That's because of my Fun Day magic!" Megan whispered to Rachel and Kirsty.

The box was full of feather boas, shiny canes and glittery top hats. The dancers looked very excited as they dived in and pulled them out. Rachel and Kirsty grinned as they saw how

thrilled Karen was to find a sparkly top hat the same colour as her new tap shoes.

She also chose a fluffy lilac boa and a shiny black cane.

"Now, girls," called Miss Henry, beaming all over her face as she put a jolly, toe-tapping tune on the CD player, "let's try these new steps. Follow me!"

Rachel, Kirsty and Megan watched as the teacher began tip-tapping her way around the room, twirling her cane. The dancers did the same, laughing as they tried to follow her. But this time, even though the steps were more complicated, they all did much better.

"Everyone's having fun!" Rachel declared, smiling to see Karen's happy face.

"Yes, I'm so glad!" Megan replied, beaming. "Thank you girls." She lifted her wand and waved at Rachel and Kirsty. "Now I must hurry and catch up on my Monday Fun Day work!"

The girls nodded.

"Goodbye, Megan!" Rachel called.

"We'll keep looking for the other Fun Day Flags!" Kirsty promised, as the little fairy blew them a kiss and zoomed away.

Rachel and Kirsty took one last look at the happy faces in the tap dancing class, grinned at each other, and then headed home for tea.

The Fun Day Fairies

Megan the Monday Fairy has got
her flag back. Now Rachel
and Kirsty must help

Tallulah the Tuesday Fairy

Win Rainbow Magic goodies!

In every book in the Rainbow Magic Fun Day Fairies series (books 36-42) there is a hidden picture of a flag with a secret letter in it. Find all seven letters and re-arrange them to make a special Fairyland word, then send it to us. Each month we will put the entries into a draw and select one winner to receive a Rainbow Magic Sparkly T-shirt and Goody Bag!

Send your entry on a postcard to Rainbow Magic Fun Day Competition, Orchard Books, 338 Euston Road, London NW1 3BH. Australian readers should write to Hachette Children's Books, Level 17/207 Kent Street, Sydney, NSW 2000. Don't forget to include your name and address. Only one entry per child. Final draw: 30th September 2007.

Have you checked out the

website at:
www.rainbowmagic.co.uk

by Daisy Meadows

The Pet Keeper Fairies

Katie the Kitten Fairy	ISBN	1 84616 166 5
Bella the Bunny Fairy	ISBN	1 84616 170 3
Georgia the Guinea Pig Fairy	ISBN	1 84616 168 1
Lauren the Puppy Fairy	ISBN	1 84616 169 X
Harriet the Hamster Fairy	ISBN	1 84616 167 3
Molly the Goldfish Fairy	ISBN	1 84616 172 X
Penny the Pony Fairy	ISBN	1 84616 171 1

The Fun Day Fairies

Megan the Monday Fairy	ISBN	1 84616 188 6
Tallulah the Tuesday Fairy	ISBN	1 84616 189 4
Willow the Wednesday Fairy	ISBN	1 84616 190 8
Thea the Thursday Fairy	ISBN	1 84616 191 6
Freya the Friday Fairy	ISBN	1 84616 192 4
Sienna the Saturday Fairy	ISBN	1 84616 193 2
Sarah the Sunday Fairy	ISBN	1 84616 194 0
Holly the Christmas Fairy	ISBN	1 84362 661 6
Summer the Holiday Fairy	ISBN	1 84362 960 7
Stella the Star Fairy	ISBN	1 84362 869 4
Kylie the Carnival Fairy	ISBN	1 84616 175 4
The Rainbow Magic Treasury	ISBN	1 84616 047 2

Coming soon:

Paige the Pantomime Fairy	ISBN	1 84616 209 2

All priced at £3.99. *Holly the Christmas Fairy, Summer the Holiday Fairy, Stella the Star Fairy* and *Kylie the Carnival Fairy* are priced at £5.99. *The Rainbow Magic Treasury* is priced at £12.99.
Rainbow Magic books are available from all good bookshops, or can be ordered direct from the publisher: Orchard Books, PO BOX 29, Douglas IM99 1BQ
Credit card orders please telephone 01624 836000
or fax 01624 837033 or visit our Internet site: www.wattspub.co.uk
or e-mail: bookshop@enterprise.net for details.

To order please quote title, author and ISBN and your full name and address.
Cheques and postal orders should be made payable to 'Bookpost plc.'
Postage and packing is FREE within the UK
(overseas customers should add £2.00 per book).
Prices and availability are subject to change.

Look out for the
Petal Fairies!

TIA THE TULIP FAIRY
1-84616-457-5

PIPPA THE POPPY FAIRY
1-84616-458-3

LOUISE THE LILY FAIRY
1-84616-459-1

CHARLOTTE THE
SUNFLOWER FAIR?
1-84616-460-5

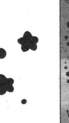

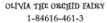

ELLA THE ROSE FAIRY
1-84616-464-8

OLIVIA THE ORCHID FAIRY
1-84616-461-3

DANIELLE THE DAISY FAIRY
1-84616-462-1

Available from
Thursday 5th April 2007

The Fun Day Fairies

For Tabitha Runchman

Special thanks to
Narinder Dhami

ORCHARD BOOKS
338 Euston Road, London NW1 3BH
Orchard Books
Hachette Children's Books
Level 17/207 Kent Street, Sydney, NSW 2000
A Paperback Original

First published in Great Britain in 2006
Rainbow Magic is a registered trademark of Working Partners Limited.
Series created by Working Partners Limited, London W6 0QT

ISBN 1 84616 188 6
1 3 5 7 9 10 8 6 4 2

Printed in Great Britain